A CHOCOLATE-BOX IRISH WEDDING

JOSIE RIVIERA

INTRODUCTION

To keep up on newly released ebooks, paperbacks, Large Print Paperbacks, audiobooks, as well as exclusive sales, sign up for Josie's Newsletter today.

As a thank you, I'll send you a Free PDF ... The Beauty Of ...

Josie's Newsletter

Did you know that according to a Yale University study, people who read books live longer?

5 STAR READER REVIEWS

"This beautifully written romance whisks the reader off to the Irish town of Wexford. High school sweethearts who had gone off to pursue their individual dreams after graduation are there to attend the wedding of her mother to his father. She is divorced and he has never married.

Is there any chance that the old spark between them can be rekindled or will the physical distance between them keep them apart despite their obvious attraction to each other? While Kiera has returned to live in Wexford, Colum teaches dance in another city.

I loved learning about some of the Irish traditions which Josie Riviera intricately weaves into this story.

This novella can easily be read in one sitting, but once again the author has found a way to make the major characters come alive within the limited number of pages.

Remember to check out the included recipe for Irish Soda Bread." - **Amazon Reviewer**

"I so enjoyed this lovely short story by Josie Riviera. I can always count on her books for a sweet romance with wonderful characters and a believable storyline when I need to escape into another world. Recommend." - **Amazon Reviewer**

"I loved this short story. He was rather reluctant to go back to his hometown for his father's wedding, but he finally decided it was the right thing to do. But would she be there?

Beautiful Keira, his first love and truthfully he had never found anyone else to replace her in his heart. He knew she had been married and had grown daughters, but did she remember? This was a sweet story to remind you that sometimes, you really can go home."- **Amazon Reviewer**

This book is dedicated to all my wonderful readers who have supported me every inch of the way.
THANK YOU!

PRAISE AND AWARDS

USA TODAY bestselling author

CHAPTER 1

*C*olum O' Brien didn't believe in Ireland's much-heralded mythology. Aye, he was Irish to the core, but there wasn't a wee bit of truth to mischievous leprechauns guarding pots of gold. Gold buried by fairies, no less. Goaded by skeptical amusement, he shook his head. He didn't put much stock in ancient Irish folklore.

Which led him to another thought: Dreams. Did they mean anything?

In any event, he wasn't looking forward to sleeping in his childhood bedroom tonight. He wondered if he'd have the same dream that had plagued him for months on end.

Over and over, just before waking, he'd gotten lost while driving on a shadowy, winding road, never finding his destination no matter how hard he tried.

Well, that assuredly wouldn't happen on this trip.

With a dismissive smile, he switched on the car radio, humming along to the folksy acoustics of "Wild Mountain Thyme," a Scottish tune.

The weather proved fine and clear for an Irish December afternoon, soon to glow with the dregs of sunset before the sky turned blue black. He opened the car window a crack, inhaling the earthy fragrance of peat smoke mingling with the bracing air of the Irish Sea. He flicked a glance toward the neighboring hills, marveling at the flicker of twinkling white lights in cottage windows—heralding the holiday season—then returned his focus to the zigzag coastal road.

A sign noted the final turnoff to a precarious, narrow two-lane road. Soon, he'd reach his family homestead in Wexford.

Thirty years ago, Colum could have accomplished this drive from his former Dublin ballet studio with one eye closed, but not anymore. His fifty-year-old eyes didn't see as well as they once did.

Unexpectedly, heavy clouds began lowering over the surrounding hay pastures. Rain spattered his windshield.

He slowed his speed. It was as if he'd driven off into a different country with no recognizable landmarks. The sudden storm had even shut off his GPS.

Where was he?

The mist thickened. Road signs became unreadable. He lowered the volume on the radio.

Instinct told him he must be nearing the last tiny village on the outskirts of Wexford. Thankfully, the taillights of another car appeared ahead.

Perhaps a long-lost relative?

Colum's widowed father had insisted on a gathering at his seaside home for his wedding celebration and asked Colum to be the best man. His father was marrying a dear friend and set a December wedding.

At first, Colum had made excuses for not attending; he taught numerous dance classes, plus was helping Sean, a troubled young man in his twenties. Years earlier, he'd met the lad at a volunteer performance in Dublin. A feature story by an American newsman, Patrick Gervez, had spotlighted how Colum's ballet troupe had given back to the city by inviting underprivileged teens to watch free productions. Since then, he'd claimed Sean as his nephew, relocated him to Farthing, and helped whenever possible.

Thus, it was difficult to get away.

This trip was an eleventh-hour decision. Not that Colum didn't love his father—though in truth, he'd been resistant to return to Wexford. The longer time passed, the more he'd lost touch with his hometown. And whenever he drove these roads, his heart remembered Keira, his high school sweetheart.

Now it was her mother who would be his father's bride.

Would Keira be there? Wexford was the last place Colum had seen her several decades earlier. But no, she lived in London now, and his father would have mentioned her attending the wedding.

Perhaps. Perhaps not. He and his father didn't converse much.

The car ahead accelerated around a sharp curve, slid off the main road, then skidded to a stop on a gravel lane.

Colum's heartbeat slowed, his fingers tightened on the steering wheel. He stomped on the brakes and swerved onto the shoulder. Quickly shutting off the engine, he dashed from his car.

As suddenly as it started, the rain quit. The clouds thinned; then slunk away.

He dragged in a breath as the driver stepped out of the car.

A woman. A fair-skinned, willowy woman. And with her came a whisper of a memory: Their shared childhood and his love for her.

"Are you all right?" Anxiety brought a tremor to his voice. Fresh breezes cooled his heated cheeks.

"I'm brilliant." She peered at him with keen blue eyes.

3

Blond hair, threaded with silver, tumbled down her back. The ends were tipped in . . . pink?

"Colum O'Brien. Is that you?" She touched a hand to her full, inviting lips—lips he well remembered.

He froze, his gaze fixed on her. He couldn't reply.

Keira Murphy. Here. He'd never expected to see her again.

"Aye. It's me." He strode closer; a tongue-tied moment.

She offered that same heart-shattering smile he'd thought about for decades.

"I'm delighted to see you, my long-lost friend," she said.

He couldn't stop gazing at her—her vivid blue eyes, sooty-black lashes and lovely slim figure. There were so many things he wanted to say, so many times he'd longed to hear her voice again.

"I'm happy to see you too." He cleared his throat. "You look grand."

More than grand. She looked exquisite.

He took both her hands in his and kissed her, a fleeting, polite brush of his lips on her cheek. Casual, yet intimate.

Her hair smelled like lilies, her skin soft and silky.

She breathed in a slight inhale, then pulled away.

He drew a shaky breath and ordered himself not to question why he'd been reduced to a long-lost friend status when they'd shared so much more.

Without another word, she moved to her car, her motions graceful. He held open the door for her and ensured she was settled. Then he headed back to his car and followed her to Wexford.

CHAPTER 2

The following morning, Keira sat in an oversized Adirondack chair on the O'Brien's spacious lawn. Moss grew on the weathered walls of the house, and the thatched roof drooped at the eaves. A string of holiday lights wound around each window, a cheerful reminder of the upcoming festivities. The scent of dew hung in the air, the grass damp from an earlier rain.

She regarded the stone markings at the front of the O'Brien property, the adjacent fields dotted by sheep, the sparkling waters of the Irish Sea.

"Hello, Keira," a deep voice called. Colum came from behind, covered her eyes with his hands, then immediately removed them. "Guess who?"

Her stomach fluttered, and she bit down on her lips to hide her smile. She admired his easy-going walk as he stepped around to face her. He was a man comfortable in his own skin, whereas she considered herself too tall and ungainly.

"That was easy," she teased. "You could've given me another minute to guess."

"I assumed you'd know it was me right away." He grinned. "May I begin our day by complimenting you, because you are gorgeous?"

"Thank you." She'd dressed in jeans and a red wool sweater, and twisted her hair back into a casual bun. She'd fussed with her appearance in anticipation of seeing him. "Were you comfortable sleeping in your childhood bedroom again?" she asked.

"The sea air is a balm. Without fail, I sleep well in Wexford." He dropped into the chair beside her and yanked out a cigarette. "It's a surprise, aye?"

"The fact you're still smoking? You vowed to quit when you were a teen."

"Over three decades later, and I constantly try to quit, although it's obvious I'm unsuccessful." He granted a rueful smile. "You never liked it."

"Still don't."

"I defer to your wishes, then." He slipped the cigarette back into his pocket, then rolled up the sleeves of his jean jacket.

"How can you dance and do that to your lungs?" As he smirked at her response, she studied him. His arms were athletic and muscular, his physique toned and fit in slim-fitting black pants and a grey knit sweater. She remembered when he'd held her at this very spot, on a similar breezy morning—a few days before she'd departed for London—a few days before New Year's Eve.

She shifted her gaze to the water. "So what's a surprise?"

"Your mum is marrying my dad," he said. "A gala event to begin the holidays."

"The best time of the year."

"Christmas?"

"And New Year's," she replied. "In fact, the entire month of December."

"The season isn't special for me . . . although I'm thankful for the adorable children I teach. The look on their faces is priceless because they're so excited."

She gestured to the O'Brien's home. The natural holly wreath hung on the back door. "We used to leave sacks by the fireplace on Christmas Eve, remember?"

"In the hopes the sacks would be filled with toys on Christmas Day." He chuckled. "Then we'd set out milk and bread on the kitchen table."

"In our house, we'd opt for a pint of Guinness and mince pies." She sighed, the memories poignant. "My mum has been alone since my father died."

"Similarly for my dad when my mum passed away."

"I recall that day." Keira had searched for Colum and discovered him sitting by the shore, his arms around his knees, his face wet with tears. At fourteen years old he'd been embarrassed she'd found him crying, for he despised weakness in himself. His shoulders were drooped, and his voice a whisper, but he'd finally relented and invited her to stay. In return, she'd offered consolation and her undying loyalty.

"Boys don't cry," he'd stated.

"But men do," she'd assured. *"Real men aren't ashamed to shed tears and show their emotions."*

"Our parents have been friends for years," Colum was saying.

"Like us." She folded her lips together. Why had she spoken the words aloud?

Until you left.

Colum hadn't uttered a sound, but, judging from his tightened expression, she could read his thoughts. They'd been inseparable. That's what happened when you were next-door neighbors.

She fingered the sleeves of her sweater. "I realize my departure from Wexford was sudden."

He shrugged.

"You know why." Too edgy to sit still, she shifted. "There were goals I wanted to accomplish before we settled down."

"Shall we give it a name?" he asked.

"What?" She sat straighter. "Me leaving?"

"Let's call it the demise of a friendship."

She flinched, as if his statement was a physical blow, even more so because of the slight catch in his tone. He'd been hurt.

For years, they'd planned to attend the same university in a neighboring town. That had only taken place for one semester. They'd pledged to stay in touch, although the busyness of life had taken hold.

"I said I would wait for you." His voice was quiet and solemn. "However, it was you who declared that we were young and couldn't plan our lives around a final commitment."

"Not once did you demand that I abandon my dreams."

"I wanted you to ride your rising career to the top," he said. "I never would've taken your achievements away."

Why? Did he love her so much that her happiness was more important than his?

She waited for him to say more. When he didn't, she searched his handsome face, although his features were remarkably bland. "You accomplished your dream," she finally said.

"Which dream was that?"

"Dancing professionally. You lifted those ballerinas effortlessly into the air. How many dancers can claim that?"

"All credited to thousands of hours of rehearsals; and workouts." He quirked a silvery-grey eyebrow. "Did you ever attend any of my performances?"

"No, not live, but I discovered YouTube."

8

He looked pleased. Something stirred in the fathomless depths of his green eyes, and her heart rate doubled.

"You watched clips?" he inquired.

"Aye."

More than clips. She'd watched his full performances.

"And you?" He shoved his hands into his pockets. "Did you find what you were looking for?"

"For a while, until I grew too old to model."

"You're not old."

"High fashion modeling is extremely competitive." The wind pushed her hair back. "When I was awarded a generous contract from an exclusive agency, I couldn't turn it down."

"And off to England you went. You hightailed it out of here before the New Year's bells rang."

She should've felt cornered by his statement—defensive. But this was Colum. She'd known him since they were children. She knew his nature. He was her constant companion, and she'd confided everything to him.

"You're asking me to apologize?" She fixed him with a level gaze. "I did on numerous occasions. How could I start our life in Wexford when London beckoned?"

"True." He watched the sea, and she followed his stare. The water was calm, the salty breeze conjuring images of picnics—wicker hampers stuffed with sausage sandwiches, sliced apples, and spice cake—while herring gulls squawked overhead.

"Fame and fortune, Kiki," he said. "Both are heady sensations."

Kiki. Her cheeks warmed. She'd nearly forgotten his nickname for her.

"I craved more." She swallowed and lifted her chin. "The excitement of a sizable city and glamorous occupation. Wexford is . . ."

He swept out his hands. "Adorable."

"You didn't stick around, either," she pointed out.

"No reason to."

Because of her? She pondered whether she should ask him. She didn't.

"I never congratulated you on your success," he went on. "Or rather, I did, but you didn't respond."

"I'm sorry. I was wrong not to answer your letters." Those precious letters—every word had broken her heart—but she couldn't write back, it would have only broken *his* heart. She'd established a new world—so different from his in only a matter of months. Nonetheless, his letters had slid from her fingers as she'd sat in her tiny London flat and wept. Joy to hear from him, bittersweet longing for leaving him behind, and the injustice of a demanding career that had initiated their separation.

She sighed. "My work was exhausting, and I hardly had a moment to breathe."

He greeted her explanation with a quick nod.

They'd been best friends. No. More than that. They'd been first loves.

"I'm standing up in the wedding." Keira navigated to a safer subject and offered a modest bow. "I'm the matron of honor."

"I'm the best man."

"Your father spoke of your obligations in Farthing," she said. "I wasn't expecting to see you."

Colum's occasional trips to Wexford over the years never had seemed to correspond with hers.

"Sean, a young lad who is like a nephew to me, continually needs my help," Colum replied. "I met him through Patrick Gervez, an American newsman who traveled to Dublin to feature a story on an outreach ballet program. Nowadays, Sean's graphic design business is doing fairly well, and he moved into his own flat. I packed his fridge with food, a matter of great importance to a twenty-something."

Typical Colum, she reflected. Forever helping people whenever possible.

"Is Sean independent?" she asked.

"He's getting there." Colum pulled his hands from his pockets and stared down at them. "I worry for him, though. I want him to be successful."

"I remember how you repeatedly volunteered at the homeless shelter in town and then organized plays for the children. You gave graciously of your expertise and talents."

"I tried."

"Help Sean, but don't give him handouts."

He grinned. "Advice now, Keira?"

"I speak from experience as a mother of two adult daughters who are often headstrong. I continued to indulge them for years, which was a mistake." She ran a hand through her hair. "Do you own a home in Farthing?"

"Renting is better for me," Colum replied. "My savings are stable, although I'm not wealthy."

"I just bought my own place."

"Congratulations! Where?"

"Take a glance to your right."

He turned. "Your mum's grand cottage?"

"She's moving in with your dad after the wedding, so, I figured, why not? It's my childhood home. Plus, I'm here to care for our parents as they age."

He leaned toward her and gave a heavy nod. "Aging is definitely a fact of everyday life, and it will be a comfort for them to have you next door."

"Their well-being is important, both physical and emotional."

"Aye." He shot a rueful grin. "And convenient when you need a cup of sugar."

"I don't bake." Keira beamed. "I sew."

"Right. How could I forget?" Colum offered a bemused chuckle. "I rang my father about my change of plans—before he requested someone else to be the best man."

"Who would he ask?"

"A cousin, maybe. Can't think of anyone who is suitable, though."

"You work in Farthing?" She'd already asked too many questions. She had at least a dozen more. She was so comfortable, so at ease conversing with him.

"I'm an instructor at Miss Clara's School of Dance," he replied. "Primarily, I teach preschoolers, and I love that age."

"Sweet ages."

"Someday, I fancy directing a public theater for adults and children."

"Underprivileged?"

"Aye, and also open to anyone in the community."

"In Farthing?"

"I haven't decided."

"You never married," she said. "Never had children."

"My longest relationship lasted all of eight months. I wasn't a particularly attentive partner while I concentrated on my career." With a noncommittal nod, he added, "Wexford was abuzz when you wed your agent in London. You were only twenty at the time."

"Henry was several years older."

"By two decades," Colum corrected. "A sophisticated man, I assume?"

Her face heated with the pain of the recollection. "He introduced me to a glittery circle. I thought of you when I met his friends at posh parties. We would've had a laugh at their uppity airs."

He grinned and leaned closer. "And your daughters are now . . ."

"Almost thirty."

"I always wanted children," he said.

"Twin daughters?"

"One would've been fine." His tone softened. "Two are better."

"Yet you never married . . ." Keira stammered with her response. When Colum studied her with those mesmerizing eyes, she forgot all rational thought. "You'll meet my girls. They're flying in from London. They'll miss the ceremony because of work, but will stay for a while afterwards."

"Through Christmas and New Year's?"

"They both have significant others in London, so I doubt it."

"I'm leaving a couple days after the service. I'm teaching several dance classes, then overseeing a holiday recital for the little ones after Christmas. The students have been preparing for months."

"You'll miss Christmas in Wexford, then. I hope to decorate my shop and my new home as soon as our parents are wed." Her brows knitted. "Will you return for New Year's?"

"Perhaps." Assiduously, he avoided her gaze.

"Remember the fun we had on New Year's Eve?"

Gently, he touched her arm. "Our families would visit for nibbles and drinks."

"And beforehand, my mum would clean the house from top to bottom."

"To signify a fresh start for the upcoming year."

"May I confess something?" she asked.

Colum automatically seemed to tense at her question. "Of course."

"On New Year's Eve, I placed a mistletoe under my pillow," she said.

"In the hopes of seeing your future partner in your

dreams." He peeked at her left hand. She'd taken her wedding band off years ago. "Is your husband . . .?"

"Henry and I divorced when our daughters finished primary school." Keira rubbed the back of her neck. "We only stayed in a polite agreement that long for the children's sake."

"Was it the right decision?"

"Each couple's choice is personal and involves many factors. From my experience, I should've left him sooner." Her marriage had been a slow deterioration of her self-confidence. As soon as her career had fallen to a standstill, Henry lost interest in her. He'd also worn away her independence and monitored her calories.

Colum glanced up and motioned toward the shore, extending a wave and a smile.

She followed his gaze to their parents. Cheryl and Richard, both in their late seventies, strolled arm and arm by the water's edge. Her mum wore a wide brimmed straw hat and billowy yellow-floral dress. Colum's father was stout and fit, as well as green-eyed, good-humored, and engaging. It gladdened Keira's heart to see their smiles. Love occurred at any age, she supposed. Just not for her.

She'd never been content in her marriage—even before Henry's verbal abuse. Had she been forever seeking the right man? She'd dated after her divorce, but no sparks.

Her chest filled with regret as she met Colum's gaze. He'd been her first love. Had he been her true love?

"Divine weather," he was saying.

"No rain in the forecast." She managed a radiant smile. "Let's hope the sun shines for the wedding."

"It's risky planning an outdoor ceremony in December," Colum noted.

"Wexford is considered the sunny southeast of Ireland. Besides, they're renting a tent with heaters for the reception. They can dash inside if need be."

"Good thing. There is constantly a threat of showers in an Irish forecast."

"Or a downpour," she inserted.

He stood and peered at the blue sky, the stretch of wispy white clouds. "Will you join me for a coffee in town? Just like we used to."

"When we were supposed to be in class."

"We'd have the craic—a good laugh and loads of fun." He chuckled. She remembered that chuckle—rich and pure and inviting. "We were a rascally pair,—ducking out of school early."

She held up a hand. "Speak for yourself."

"Hah! Half the time, you'd initiate our adventures. We'd pool our lunch money, hop on a bus, and eventually land at Michael D's whiling away the afternoon over scones and coffee and homework."

"Homework?"

He smiled. "Once in a while."

"I dine at Michael D's often."

His smile wavered. "I'm trying to get my head around the fact that all this time I assumed you still lived in London."

"I own a dressmaker's shop a few doors down from Michael D's," she explained. "In fact, I designed my mum's wedding dress. Care to take a peek?"

"Isn't it bad luck to see the bride's dress before the wedding?"

"Only if you're the groom." She accepted his extended hand and got to her feet. "Don't take any photos to show your dad."

"You're the one who could never keep a secret. Chatterbox."

She gave his shoulder a playful nudge as they began walking. "And you were quiet."

"So many memories." Conflicting emotions flashed across

his well-defined features—his sharp cheekbones that reminded her of a proud Roman warrior. His gaze locked with hers, a silent communication. He knew her so well. She'd never been at a loss for words, and they'd sit for hours. Colum, attentive and encouraging, while she chatted endlessly. She'd become a famous designer, and he'd continue volunteering and open a performing arts school. Perhaps they'd marry in the winter. A Christmas wedding, or New Year's . . .

Their lives had taken such different paths.

But what if . . .

No, no, no. She refused to play the "what if" game.

"What's the name of your shop?" Colum asked.

"Keira's Wexford Boutique."

They stepped onto a stone path, lingering to appreciate the buds of holly and pansies blooming up from the cold ground.

"You loved fashion." Colum paused to pick a bouquet, handing the flowers to her. "You made me a shirt once."

She sniffed, savoring the fragrant scent. He'd frequently slip her a spray of cowslip or clover or shamrocks—depending on the season.

"I sewed the shirt from jersey cotton fabric and a pre-made sewing pattern," she replied. "It was tight on you."

"I wore it often."

"Only so you wouldn't hurt my feelings."

He'd ignored teasing from the other boys and had worn her handmade shirt with pride. He constantly looked out for her. Her protector. He wanted to make her happy.

"You sewed this for me, Kiki?" he'd asked with a broad smile when she'd presented it to him. *"It's brilliant."*

He'd tugged it over his dog-eared t-shirt. He was tanned and muscular by then—on the cusp of adulthood—nearing eighteen.

The shirt hadn't been brilliant—an amateur's attempt at sewing and design—boasting a bold Hawaiian pattern of multicolored birds and leaves. Nevertheless, her interest in fashion, encouraged by Colum, had thrived.

"Is your shop successful?" He stood so close, the warmth of his skin heated her own. She inhaled the crisp scent of the sea. Knowing him, he'd probably gone for a swim at sunup.

He still had the muscular build of his younger self, his profile lithe, yet solid. His eyes were a mossy green— reminding her of the color of the forest after a hard rain. His hair was salt and pepper, raked short and side-swept.

"I'm happy," she acknowledged. "I've come to realize this idyllic wee town is my home. For me, happiness constitutes success."

"Ahh, living in Wexford."

She frowned. "Is there a problem?"

"Little towns are ideal for many chaps." He exhaled. "However, the country character here, coupled with my recollections of the old ways . . ."

"You find fault with our traditions? Our folklore?"

"Some of it. Nevertheless, a large city offers more theater and restaurant choices." He winked. "Plus, no one remembers me as an awkward adolescent."

"You were a pro in every sport. Whereas I—all legs and arms—"

CHAPTER 3

"*Y*ou're exquisitely perfect." Colum blurted the words before he could stop himself. He scanned Keira's delicate profile—the curve of her nose, her flawless complexion with a sprinkling of freckles, and heard the sincerity in her tone. She actually didn't realize how attractive she was.

However, her blue eyes shone with a spirit that hadn't been diminished by hardship.

Her youthful features had matured, fulfilling the certainty of loveliness, enriched with a mellowness that had developed with maturing. Her posture was straight, her figure slender.

His only desire was to touch her, kiss her, cherish the delightful feelings intensifying inside him—the first true emotions he'd felt in decades.

He cupped her cheek. "Numerous points in my life have reminded me of you. I wondered if our mutual memories ever caused you to smile."

He braced himself for her reply. When she finally dragged her gaze to his, she drew a wobbly breath. "I laughed a lot in London whenever I remembered our adventures."

He bent his head and his lips grazed hers. So delicious, so inviting. "You're my precious Kiki," he murmured. "You've been my forever—"

"No." She tugged free. Her complexion was flushed, her eyes wet. "You're leaving in a few days."

"Aye, but there's no reason why I can't return. I've never stopped thinking about you." He brushed the shiny hair from her forehead and grinned at the pink highlighted tips. In her teens she'd been the town nonconformist, experimenting with bizarre fashions. However, the bright makeup and outlandish feather hats had never diminished the beauty of her high cheekbones and expressive eyes. No wonder a London modeling agency had signed her on the spot.

"Words are easy, Colum." He respected the proud grace of her walk as she stepped away. "Circumstances may prevent a person from following through—no matter their intentions."

When they reached her driveway, Keira insisted on driving them to town, vowing to take the curves slowly in light of the previous evening's mishap. She didn't. If anything, she accelerated during the ten-minute drive, while he gripped the edge of the passenger seat. When they arrived at her shop, she rummaged in her handbag for the keys.

He squinted through the wavy glass window of the vacant building next door. The exterior paint flaked at random, the interior was dust-coated, the walls cracked.

"What business was here previously?" Colum asked.

"Nothing for years," she answered. "There was talk of converting the space into a high-class hotel, but the funds never came through."

She finally found the key, and they stepped inside her shop.

It was tidy and spotless, and scents of cedar and mint lingered in the air. Clothes racks sported fine woolens and tweeds, hand knit scarves and cable stitch cream sweaters tagged to sell.

"Do you employ a staff?" he asked.

"Recently, I hired a mother and her adult daughter. They're smart, efficient, and excellent seamstresses." Keira walked to a back room and brought out a knee-length lace dress in a champagne shade, along with a flowered crown headpiece. She illustrated how she'd sewn each delicate button by hand.

"Tasteful for your mum." He applauded. "May I ask what the daughter of the bride is wearing?"

Keira winked. "It's a surprise."

"In secondary school, I'd ask what you planned to wear the following day, and you'd consistently say—"

"It's a surprise," they chimed in unison.

"Why did you forever ask me the same question, Colum?"

"To prepare myself." He attempted to keep his features straight. "I never knew what newfangled outfit you'd come up with."

"Fashion is fun. An adventure."

He rolled his eyes. "You found enough for both of us." He'd willingly gone anywhere she'd dragged him and felt fortunate just to be with her.

"I wished to dress better than those pretty girls in school who flirted with you," she said.

He chucked her under the chin. "I believe you were jealous."

"Believe whatever suits you."

"Were you . . . jealous?" He drew her near, held her close. He couldn't help himself. His yearning for her slowed his breathing.

As he gazed into her eyes, the seconds paused—becoming the shared remembrances of delightful hours, of days, of years.

He'd sought to deny it, but he'd never been able to resist her. When they were young, they'd fallen into an easy friendship—enjoyable and uncomplicated. By their teens, their relationship had changed. Romance began to bloom—although they'd both resisted the attraction to each other.

For decades afterward, his thoughts had gravitated toward her. How was she faring in London? Had she forgotten him? Undoubtedly, because she was married.

But now they were reunited, and the seasons apart were a mere moment in time.

"Jealous? Don't be ridiculous. You flatter yourself." Keira fussed with a tweed cape on a hanger, fumbling with the fabric. "The programs you choreographed at the Wexford homeless shelter were fun and uplifting, and you were only in your teens."

"Thank you. I love working with children." He wanted to congratulate her on navigating the subject change so seamlessly.

She turned toward him. "Do you still dance and perform?"

"There aren't many roles for fifty-something males," he replied.

"You were a key dancer with the Dublin ballet."

"Until I reached thirty. Then the younger, ambitious men were happy to replace me."

"Same in my occupation." She went back to fussing with the cape. "Runway models are most successful between the ages of sixteen and twenty-one."

"And afterwards?"

"I did catalogues. And sewing to make ends meet while raising two daughters."

"You're exceptional, Kiki. You lived on your own in London."

Tears welled in her eyes. He didn't expect them.

"My ex-husband, Henry, considered me obsolete when I aged out of working the runway." The cape fell off the hanger. She bent to pick it up. "After our divorce, I continued to question my self-worth."

"Did he abuse you?

"Not physically. His abuse was emotional." She lifted her hands, then let them drop. "I should've divorced him sooner, but I was trapped. Two young daughters and no way to support us."

"Now you're successful and content."

"I am." She laughed, unforced and laid-back. "This tiny slice of the world is my lifeline, and I'm not relocating anytime soon."

Life in a microscopic town was ideal for some people, just not for him. He dismissed the unspoken thought and sought a more manageable topic. Absently, he fingered a velvet hanger, while he relished spending the day with her. Finally, the Keira he recognized was emerging from behind her careful wall. Honestly explaining her hardships, without sugarcoating what he'd imagined had been her opulent London lifestyle.

"Ready to lead the way to Michael D's?" he suggested.

"Considering the coffee shop is a few doors down, it's not difficult."

"Do they still serve tea cakes?"

"Aye. And buttered scones with strawberry jam. Your favorite. The new owner kept the same menu."

He patted his stomach. "Your mum baked superb scones with lemon curd and whipped cream. You brought them to me after my ballet practice, rolled up in foil and topped with a silver bow."

"She still bakes over a turf fire. Batches of soda bread sit on our kitchen counter as I speak."

"Thus a delightful afternoon awaits."

She narrowed her gaze. "Colum O'Brien, you can't sample desserts and bread all day."

"Watch me." He laced his fingers through hers and led her out of the shop.

They passed McKay's jewelers and peered through the display case window. As was customary in many of Ireland's shops, the Claddagh Ring took center stage.

"Love, loyalty, and friendship." Keira admired an array of sterling silver and gold bands.

"Did your mum hand her wedding ring down to you?"

"I married in London, and she didn't attend because my father was sick. He died a year later, and she continued to wear the ring on her right hand. Now that she's marrying your father, she placed it in her bedroom drawer for safe-keeping."

Colum hooked his arm around her shoulders. "Awaiting you."

"I won't marry again."

"Why ever not?" he asked.

"Once was enough. I'm obviously not good at marriage." Her tone thickened, and she clasped her hands together. "Perhaps one of my daughters will wear it someday."

He swallowed the dull ache in his throat. He could still visualize Keira planning their future all those years ago.

"And after we graduate from university, Colum, we'll marry," she'd declared. Her color was high, her joy bubbling and infectious. *"Won't it be grand?"*

"Aye." He'd cradled her in his arms. *"Grand, indeed."*

CHAPTER 4

When they reached the O'Brien's cottage, Keira invited Colum into her home. The comforting scent of buttermilk and raisins and freshly baked Irish soda bread greeted him as they entered the light-filled kitchen. The walls were painted a dove gray, and a bold patterned rug covered the ancient tiled floor. Photographs littered a side bureau. Several were black and white photos of him and Keira. In one, they stood by the shore. He displayed a wiggling fish—their only catch that day—while she beamed, her light-blond hair in a long braid over her shoulder, and proudly held up the fishing pole. They were eight years old.

Keira gestured to the loaves stacked beneath numerous glass containers. "All ready for the reception."

"Your mum shouldn't bake for her own wedding."

"Why not? Baking is therapy."

He lifted a lid. "May I?"

"Sure. I'll slice a loaf and brew a pot of tea."

A few minutes later, she poured two steaming cups of robust breakfast tea and combined loads of milk and sugar into her cup. Once she settled, he seated across from her. The expansive bay window boasted an unobstructed view of the craggy hills and sea beyond.

"Thus, our parents are out and about today," he said.

"They drove to Waterford." Keira set the white porcelain teapot on the table. "My mum wished to speak with the DJ in person."

Colum sat back in joking amazement. "No bagpipes tomorrow?"

"The piper will perform when guests arrive and leave the ceremony." She sipped her tea and gazed at him over the rim of her cup. "At the reception, she insists on traditional Irish folk music."

Colum lifted his teacup in a salute. "She is a wise woman."

"I agree. She allowed me to make my own mistakes." Keira poured more tea. "The rehearsal begins in a couple hours, and the pastor arrives at five o'clock."

"What rehearsal?"

"We'll practice walking in and out, and where we'll stand during the ceremony. Didn't your father mention anything?"

Colum drummed his fingers on the wooden table. "Men don't talk much."

"My mum requested that you and I plan an impromptu party for afterwards."

"Did she now?" he asked. "I could do with more warning."

"Are you busy?"

"Not at all."

"Good." Keira smiled. She was gorgeous when she smiled. Her face was all gentle curves, her silky hair tumbling over her shoulders. "I'll ring a few places in town."

She made quick work of the arrangements, then picked up their tea cups and placed them in the sink. After she finished, she remained silent for a beat.

"When, exactly, do you return to Farthing?" she inquired.

The anticipation of a commitment was unmistakable. The speculation of "what If" he didn't have to leave.

But he did. He'd created another life. He leased a flat and had resided in Farthing for ages.

He traced his fingers along the sides of her face and smoothed back her blond hair. She turned her cheek nearer his palm before she slipped away.

Did his remembrances of their former years—when they'd finished each other's sentences—bring her the same pangs of heartfelt longing? He'd presumed his reminiscences were embellished by the idealism of youth. Now he wasn't so sure.

"My preschoolers await my return," he said.

"Do you enjoy teaching the younger age group?"

"Absolutely. I use distraction and positive feedback. And I heap on the compliments when the children point their toes."

"Do they . . . point their toes?"

"Hardly ever." He grinned as she laughed out loud.

Keira's radiance brightened his mood. When he'd lost his mum, he'd wept, his sorrow unbearable. Keira had been there —quietly consoling, encouraging him to express his grief. She'd put aside her sewing that day, changed her plans. Comrades till the end, they'd vowed. They'd sat tight for hours until the sky darkened.

He was her priority, she'd assured him. As she'd been his.

"My American friends, Patrick and Cora Gervez, have flown to Ireland for a holiday," Colum continued. "He's the newsman who introduced me to Sean in Dublin. In any case, I want to show him and his wife, Cora, around Farthing. As soon as the recital is over, I'll return to Wexford."

"Is that a promise?"

"A promise and then some." He kissed her temple. "That is, unless you're traveling somewhere for New Year's Eve?"

"Have you forgotten, Colum?" Lightly, she stroked his hand. Or maybe he stroked hers. "I'm not going anywhere."

CHAPTER 5

*A*lthough rehearsal dinners in Ireland weren't standard, Keira opted for a casual soiree with hors d'oeuvres, oysters, and pints of beer at sunset. They arranged tables and chairs under a canopied pergola on the sandy beach, and Colum and his father built a smoldering bonfire between the sand dunes. The fire whispered hisses, the flames flickering, and the air smelled of smoke and pine.

Bottles of water were plentiful, along with a marble board laden with a wheel of moist blue cheese, sharp cheddar, goat's cheese, soda crackers and crusty baguettes.

Keira reached for a handful of grapes as she admired the blade-leaf potted plants adorning the tables. The men had secured strings of subdued vintage light bulbs to the pergola.

Colum came to stand beside her, his arm brushing hers. He wore slim-fitting swimming trunks and a striped polo shirt, and his smile enhanced his good-looking face.

"May I?" he asked.

"May you what?" Her chest surged with excitement. She couldn't refute the unmistakable magnetism whenever he neared, as if an electrical arc sizzled between them.

He touched a finger to his bottom lip, a teasing gesture she fondly recalled. "May I have your grapes?"

"There's plenty where these came from, and I can assure they're all the same." She motioned toward the tables. "We requested the caterer bring fresh figs and dried apricots too. Remember?"

"You did most of the arranging."

"Correction. *All* the arranging."

"Right." Her remark earned a chuckle. "Well, I'd prefer your grapes."

"You constantly stole my food when we were young."

He swept an arm around her waist. "Not stealing. I asked first."

With an exaggerated sigh, she handed him the grapes. "Help yourself."

"I'd like nothing better than to help myself . . . to a kiss." His soft breath brushed her cheek. His green eyes smoldered as he bent his head and pressed his lips on hers.

The kiss deepened, and she wound her hands around his shoulders.

Somewhere near the house, her mum called. Colum broke the kiss, and an unexpected loneliness filled Keira's heart. With a sigh, she encouraged herself to yield to reason. Too many years had passed. Was it too late to start their romance again—simply pick up where they left off?

A possibility. But life, she'd discovered, was seldom simple. Twists and turns were encountered around every bend.

She plucked his arm from her waist and turned. "We're coming, mum," she called back.

Colum held her hand as they started toward the house. "I always admired your generous nature," he said.

"As if I had a choice," she joked.

He polished off her entire sprig of grapes and they shared a laugh.

He had laugh lines now. So did she.

As they walked, she reflected on their day. She liked sitting at the kitchen table with him and planning a rehearsal dinner celebration. She liked everything about this charming man with rock solid arms and sturdy shoulders.

"My two favorite young people," her mum declared when Keira and Colum approached. "You make a stunning couple."

"We're hardly a couple," Keira replied. "And we're hardly young."

Colum's father strode over. "Could've fooled me on both counts."

Their smiling approval was so contagious that Keira couldn't curb her grin.

"Your mum and my father are wise." Colum followed his declaration with a throaty laugh. She glanced at him, startled to see the love shining in his eyes, and her heart soared.

After chatting about the wedding and wishing their parents "good night," Colum kept his fingers firmly around Keira's and led her to the waterfront.

Those who chose to swim after the rehearsal had been encouraged to wear their swimsuits, and Keira had arranged a basket of towels on the beach. The full moon rose, a deep silver disc, steady and true, much like the fine-looking man smiling down at her.

Colum gestured with his chin. "Lots of folks are enjoying the water this evening. Are you up for a swim?"

"They're mental. The sea is freezing."

He chuckled. "It'll get even colder in January."

She pointed to the waves slicing across the rocks. "Is your judgement clouded? Have you been drinking?

"I don't drink alcohol."

She knew that about him. He'd never changed.

A sparkle lit his eyes. "We Irish are a hardy people."

"Uh, huh."

"Invariably, I swam faster once we reached our teens."

"Invariably?" She placed her hands on her hips, her legs slightly apart. "Is your fancy word a dare?"

"Absolutely." He shrugged off his shirt. His chest was firm and well-defined. Graceful and compelling. A man who devoted his life striving for beauty and artistry.

"As you may recall," she said, "I'm an exceptional swimmer."

"You should be." Wryly, he grinned. "You live by the sea."

She bumped up against him. "So did you." She untied her white shimmer lace coverup and set it on a chair. Her vivid-purple swimsuit sported a sweetheart neckline and revealed a peek of fair skin.

His admiring stare wasn't lost on her and her cheeks heated.

He grabbed her hand, and they dashed into the frigid water—the spray soaking their faces. Total immersion brought her teeth to chattering within minutes. They splashed each other before Keira admitted defeat and they headed for shore.

Colum snatched several thick towels and wrapped one around her. He arranged another on the sand close to the bonfire and beckoned her to sit.

With a lightness in her limbs, she obliged.

He sat beside her, tucked the towel nearer her shoulders, and cuddled her. Bits of sand clung to his cheeks, and she brushed it off.

"I would've stayed in the water longer," he declared.

"Uh, huh." She still shivered, but the heat of the fire, the warmth of Colum's body, offered pure pleasure. "Then why are your lips blue?"

"Yours are bluer." A relaxed smile worked across his

features. She recalled how his eyes darkened whenever he'd contemplated kissing her after a swim, and her pulse quickened. The scent of salt water and his damp skin brought wants and misgivings.

He bent his head, cupped her face and kissed her with aching tenderness. Oh, the taste of him, the gentleness of an unstoppable kiss. She didn't want it to end—like their youthful declarations. Only her emotions were different now. Deeper and sounder.

She pressed her forehead against his chest, her hands flattened on his shoulders. "I wish you could stay in Wexford permanently," she whispered. "This is your home."

"For many years, but not anymore." He gathered a deep breath. "In all honesty, I can't risk being hurt again."

"You're referring to me?"

"Aye."

She blinked, focusing on his words. "I wouldn't do that." She drew back, attempting to understand the overwhelming emotions he awakened in her. Had she hidden behind outward merriment and animation in London—a vigilant emotional balance that numbed her feelings? She'd clung to that balance for years, thankful for her two cherished daughters to love and care for.

"I realize you wouldn't intentionally." Colum kissed her forehead. "Though, please understand that my heart can only take so much."

She went to stand, and he kept his arm firmly around her. "May I hold you a while longer?"

Why? He'd hedged about continuing their relationship. Maybe he'd never been interested. Still, his affectionate smile melted her insides, and she relaxed. She regarded him and fingered the greying hairs at his temple. His lashes were black and spiky, his features well-defined.

She stirred, and he drew her closer, and the instinctively

protective gesture prompted her to smile. He buried his face in her hair, and she leaned back and briefly squeezed her eyes closed. Two people reconnecting on a windswept Irish beach. Two sweethearts. Tonight, she felt wholly at peace with herself, and in seamless accord with the universe.

"There's a family of otters. I saw them earlier when I took a swim. And kingfishers." He pointed toward the water, a sheet of indigo-blue silk. The moon rose higher, reflecting a milky glow across the hills. A chorus of crickets and the sizzling pops of the fire serenaded them, the murmurs of the departing guests fading away. "Do you recall when we'd spend the day intent on spotting an otter?"

"Aye. You'd spin their water frolics into fairy tales." Her throat clogged with tears. She inhaled a deep breath to compose herself.

"Once upon a time," he'd often recited in their youth, *"there was a girl named Kiki, and a guy named Colum."*

A fairytale. A happily ever after.

What happiness had she missed while she'd worn blinders —all to achieve success in a fickle career?

THE FOLLOWING morning dawned pleasant and clear. Keira drew open her lace curtains and gazed out her second-floor bedroom window, smirking as her mum directed the workers on the placement of the large white tent and the cathedral windows on the sidewalls. Colum's father guided other workmen on the location of the portable heaters.

Further down the shore, Colum emerged from the water. His swimming trunks draped low on his hips, his muscular chest glistened with drops of water. The sun glinted behind him, outlining his athletic physique.

He slung a towel around his neck and padded over to their parents.

Watching him, Keira's thoughts emptied of everything except him.

He raised his head, as if he felt her gaze.

"Aren't you chilly?" she teased.

He gave a look of lighthearted superiority. "Not a bit."

"You aren't serious. The temperature of the water is fifty degrees Fahrenheit."

"In truth, I'm frozen."

Her shout of hilarity almost drowned out his next remark.

"Can't wait to see what you'll wear to the wedding, Kiki," he said.

Kiki again.

She ignored the unexpected knot in her chest. Or, at least, she tried. A memory of their mutual years flashed through her mind—holding hands at sunset, shared secrets in the dark. Despite her anticipation of an exciting lifestyle beyond Wexford, she couldn't pretend the flood of emotions whenever he was near didn't exist.

"It'll bring tears to your eyes," she called back.

She assumed she'd moved on with her life. She hadn't. For decades, she'd searched to fill the void in her heart. And she'd fallen in love, once again, with the man she'd left behind.

AN HOUR LATER, Keira donned a knee-length, carnation red dress with a polka-dotted sash that she'd fashioned and sewn. The ends of her hair boasted a ruby hue, and she styled her heavy curls to the side with a pearl clip. She opted for braided jute sandals, satisfied that her outfit was tasteful and sensible.

As she gazed at her reflection in her full-length mirror, she recalled the conversation with her mum from the previous evening, after Keira and Colum had parted.

She'd knocked on Keira's bedroom door and entered. "I wanted to speak to you about Colum," she'd begun. "Day in and day out through the years, you looked splendid as a couple, but especially tonight."

"We're great friends."

"So you've made known. Nonetheless, I see the way he looks at you."

"I haven't noticed anything of the sort," Keira had replied.

"He can't stop staring, and you dissolve whenever you meet his gaze."

"He's leaving in mere days."

"Encourage him to stay. You've never gotten over each other. The sooner you both admit the truth, the better."

Her mother had known how difficult it was for Keira to leave him and Wexford all those decades ago. It hadn't been an easy decision.

"He has work and obligations in Farthing," Keira replied.

Even now, she longed for the tenderness of his embrace, the gentle insistence of his kiss. She'd appreciated the precious hours they'd spent in each other's company, and she sensed Colum felt the same. But what would tomorrow evening bring? Or the following? Would they finally celebrate a New Year's side by side again?

All those decades ago, she'd departed the day after Christmas, intent on securing a flat in London before her modeling contract began the first of January.

"New Year's is symbolic, Kiki," Colum had explained. They'd spent every holiday never more than a stone's throw from each other. *"Let's reflect on the past year, then look forward."*

By the time they were teens, they'd toasted, their sparkling grape juice glasses clinking as they cozied in Colum's living room by a fire in the hearth, while their parents celebrated at the local pub. They'd return well before midnight and switch the television on for a communal countdown.

"Why do folks insist on coming in the front door, then leaving out the back door?" Keira had asked him.

"It's touted to bring good luck." His lips had deepened into an exasperated smile. *"Another one of Ireland's traditions."*

Laughing, she'd refuted, *"Many traditions have a purpose behind them. Rituals are performed for hundreds of years, although few folks can recall why."*

His look implied a struggle between seriousness and humor. *"Here's a tradition that will last. Come what may, we'll spend New Year's with one another every year."*

Keira blinked back tears at the remembrance. That was the last New Year's she'd seen him.

"Sometimes the pathway to the person you cherish is a twisty and lengthy road," her mum was saying. Her eyes had misted, although her smile offered encouragement.

Keira snapped up her bouquet, a fragrant mix of snapdragons and sunflowers, then walked to the window. Laughing and chatting, in a kaleidoscope of vibrant dresses and navy suits, ushers were seating the guests in rows of white chairs facing the sea. The pastor fixed himself at the altar, a classic wooden archway decorated with purple sea asters.

Her veins tingled with excitement at the enthusiasm of the guests. Today was a glorious, sunny day, the rugged landscape dusted with snow on the highest mountain peaks. The stark blue skies promised joyfulness and enchantment.

At noon, the ceremony began with a lone bagpiper playing Mendelssohn's Wedding March. A ripple went through the crowd as Keira and Colum took their places, and the bride walked down the aisle to her groom.

Her mum's champagne lace dress complemented her rosy complexion. The flowered crown headpiece brought a statement of romance to her wavy gray hair. Her closely set blue eyes brimmed with happiness.

Colum's father, dressed in a black notched tuxedo, stood ruddy faced and noble, beaming as his bride approached.

Keira gazed at the two men, father and son. Their resemblance was astounding. The square jawlines and eye color were the same, as were their natures. Attentive and charismatic, both men forever wore a smile.

"You're beautiful," Colum said softly to her. His green eyes glistened with tears.

Her stomach flipped and she smiled—craving all things Colum. The boy he was, and the man he'd become.

Behind him, the sea shimmered—sparkles under the sun. In her teens, she'd imagined the shimmers as magical fairy dust, and that the magic would lead to an enchanted life with him.

After the wedding, they'd sing and dance at the reception. The lively melody of Galway Girl, an Irish tune. Or a romantic waltz, and he'd hold her in his arms.

Her pulse thrummed with the anticipation of another day with him.

She'd suggest he stay a wee bit longer. She wanted him to meet her daughters. She was so proud of them.

"All Those Endearing Young Charms," closed the ceremony. The emotional lyrics about a woman's youth fading away, encouraged the guests to join in.

Dozens offered congratulations, circling the bride and groom as they stepped toward the tent. Traditional Irish pub fare—hearty fish and chips, shepherd's pie, and seafood chowder, would be served buffet-style.

Keira caught up to Colum, who was speaking on his cellphone. His eyebrows crinkled in concern.

"Are you coming?" she asked.

He clicked off the phone. "I can't. I must leave."

"Now?"

"The young man in Farthing I told you about—"

"Sean? You loaded up his refrigerator."

Colum rubbed his jaw. "He hit a rough patch and was thrown out of his flat."

"He recently moved in."

"Correct, but he needs me. Patrick Gervez and his wife, Cora, are also in Farthing. They flew over from America for a visit to Ireland in the wintertime."

"Can't they handle Sean's problems?"

"They're on holiday. They're good friends, but Sean is my responsibility."

"He really isn't."

"He is, though." Colum's tone was strained, his chin high. "I won't shirk my obligation and ask my American friends to shoulder my burdens. I'll extend my congratulatory wishes to our parents and go pack."

What obligation? she thought. You're not even technically related. I need you too.

She respected that Colum always placed the welfare of others before himself, but she wanted him to be a part of her life too.

"Then . . . this is goodbye?" she asked aloud.

"Kiki, I've been thinking. Maybe it's better this way." He strode closer, his gaze locked on hers. "Our friendship has lasted decades, and neither of us can ignore our first love. But we shouldn't complicate our relationship with anything else."

Like romance? Like love? Like kisses under the moonlight?

Her vision blurred, her chest ached. "Aye. Friends till the end." She swiveled. She wouldn't let him see her cry. Keeping her shoulders straight, she quickened her pace to the tent.

She remained out of sight when Colum got into his car a

few minutes later. He'd changed into jeans and a button down blue shirt, and shrugged on a jacket. For a moment he waffled, glancing around.

"I'm right here," she was tempted to shout. But she didn't, and the stab of regret pierced deeper as he drove away. She'd never see his lopsided smile, nor hear his easy-going chuckle, again.

HER MUM APPEARED—KEIRA wasn't sure when.

"He left early because someone needed him." Tears clogged Keira's throat. She trembled, despite the sun's warmth.

"He apologized for his hasty departure. He always was the first in line to come to everyone else's aid." She gave Keira's hand a mild squeeze. "You'll see him again."

When? Keira's fingers were cold, but her mum didn't seem to mind.

CHAPTER 6

*T*wo weeks later, and the day after Christmas, Colum flicked warning glances at his four-year-old ballerina students, but they paid him no heed. They knew he was a marshmallow when it came to disciplining them. Dressed in pink tights and black leotards, their hair tugged back in classic buns, they raced around his studio like it was a preschool gym. They should've been practicing their pitter patter turns by the barre. Instead, they practiced . . . running.

He clapped his hands to bring their attention to him. Alas, no such luck. He hunkered down to tie a tiny ballet slipper, reminded them to work at their dances for the upcoming recital, and then shepherded them to their waiting parents.

After speaking assurances to several anxious mothers, and thanking them for bringing their children for a last-minute practice, he arranged his gear in his locker and leaned his head against the wall. Since resuming his everyday life, he'd grown weary of the town of Farthing—and even his surrogate nephew.

After attending a morning church service the day before, their Christmas dinner had consisted of takeout boxty, potato pancakes stuffed with meat and vegetables. For the remainder of the day, Colum had volunteered at a soup kitchen while his nephew created a custom logo for a local shop.

In addition, Colum's dreams had started again—driving on a shadowy road and being lost.

He grasped a cigarette, then shoved it back into his pocket. He craved a coffee, or tea . . . but he'd have to sit in traffic forever first. In Wexford, everything was a mere ten minutes away.

"I dine at Michael D's often," Keira had declared.

Keira—eternally in his heart, eternally in his mind. He'd assumed he was over her. He'd assumed he'd secured her in a safe, secret place. Returning to Wexford had been bittersweet, but memories of her and their years together had struck him at every turn. He'd even jogged along the beach the morning after his arrival and discovered the oak tree where they'd carved their initials when they were twelve.

But in a forty-eight-hour period, how could he reunite with his teenage sweetheart? He was a bachelor in his fifties and wasn't about to leave everything he'd worked so hard for, to move back to his hometown. Plus, could he truly contemplate settling down?

He blew out a breath. He'd tried to forget her. If anything, his feelings had grown stronger.

With a cheery nod to the straggling parents, he shrugged on his twill jacket and exited the studio.

Restless, he wandered the bustling city streets as people hurried home from work. Bright icicle lights illuminated the shops, and aromatic pine filled the air. Daylight had dwindled, and a purple dusk came earlier than expected. The days, the years, passed too quickly, and each hour was precious.

He paused. So what was he doing in Farthing?

He'd told himself not to care, citing a myriad of reasons, expecting his feelings would fade.

She'd left at eighteen, and he'd been devastated. Nevertheless, he loved her—a love so powerful it exploded within him. Surely, she felt the same.

He needed to take the right path and find his way home. Back to Keira and Wexford.

He drew out his cellphone to contact his father, then Keira's mum.

He hesitated.

Texts were a start. In person was better.

Decision made, he rang Sean, and offered his flat to sublet. Colum had secured a part-time job to enable Sean to get his finances in order and hoped the lad would be responsible. He'd shared his knowledge and been a sounding board. Now was a chance for the young man to transition to independence.

Then Colum enlisted the help of his father and Keira's mum.

Next came a phone call to Patrick Gervez and his wife, Cora, inviting them to visit the southern part of Ireland and Colum's hometown for a special event.

His fourth request was to Clara, his employer and longtime friend. She assured she'd find a suitable teacher replacement, that the recital would go off without a hitch, and encouraged Colum to follow his heart.

His heart. He pressed a hand to his chest.

He hurried to his flat to attend to last-minute details and pack a suitcase.

Then he drove to Wexford as if his life depended on it.

CHAPTER 7

*K*eira wrapped her fingers around a fresh mug of tea, leaned back in the oversized Adirondack chair on the O'Brien's lawn, and gazed at the blue-grey ripples of the water, a reflection of the sky. Today, she wore a one-piece V-neck jumpsuit, a snuggly knit in a bold fuchsia, and draped a thick woolen cape over her shoulders to ward off the chill.

The end of December carried a chilly, overcast day, and the holiday had occurred in a blur. Colum had texted every day—and they'd kept the topics neutral.

After a Christmas church service in town, she'd prepared roast turkey, stuffing, and buttery carrots, and dined with their parents. Colum had phoned, wishing them all a "Merry Christmas." He'd perfected his friendly, amiable tone.

Her eyes burned, but she didn't blame it on the smoke from the turf fires.

She blamed it on the tears she'd shed since he'd departed. All that remained were precious snapshots of their youth that she safeguarded in her mind. Many years ago, he'd unknowingly set the bar high. His likable character, wit, and intelligence had become the standard she'd unwittingly measured every man by since. They were so compatible—pieces of a puzzle fitting in perfect agreement.

"Hello, Kiki, my love," a deep, beloved voice came from behind her.

She gasped. The shattering gentleness of Colum's words sent a jolt through her.

She set her mug on the grass and slowly rose. Now he stood in front of her—his tall frame clad in dark jeans, a flannel shirt, and his familiar twill jacket. She assumed she was still breathing. She couldn't be sure.

"Colum." Her thoughts reeled. His presence was a solid force, mesmeric and undeniable. "Why . . . why are you here?"

"I missed you." His tone was whispered, raw with emotion. "And, I'm here to stay. Do you know any place for rent?"

"In Wexford?" Her gaze lifted to the man who held her heart. "For whatever reason?"

"For you. Only for you." He captured her in his arms. His lips pressed hungrily with an aching desire that would forever remain in her memory.

She molded nearer to him. "I've missed you too." Their breaths mingled. She returned his kiss with all the yearning in her soul.

His hands slid up and down her back. "I came to tell you that I love you. Everything you do—everything you say—everything you represent."

The taste of his lips brought unbearable happiness. She didn't want him to stop, fearful he might disappear.

"My precious Kiki, you're goodness, decency, and all that's true in the world," he said. "You're the treasure of my life."

She pressed a trembling finger to his mouth. "And you're

the treasure of mine." Heat radiated through her body. Her heartbeat raced so loud, surely he heard it.

Tears glistened at the corner of his eyes as he kept her firmly in his embrace. "I was fearful of having my heart broken anew and ordered myself not to love you."

She wiped away his tears. "And?"

"It didn't work." He cradled her face in his hands. "When we were apart, I realized we'd missed out on love once, and I won't allow it to happen again."

"I can't believe you're here. I'm speechless."

"All I need is a single word." He pulled a small black velvet box from his pocket and handed it to her.

She opened the box, which revealed a sterling Claddagh ring. "When did you—?"

"The ring is your mum's. She's a grand woman."

Keira ran her palm along the gleaming silver. The crown symbolized loyalty, friendship, and the heart represented love. Tenderness pulsed through her. He'd returned, determined to recover the love they'd begun decades earlier.

"Do you like it?" In his eagerness, his features appeared almost boyish.

"Nothing can ever mean more."

"If you don't . . . I'll buy you a new ring, although it's bad luck."

"You don't believe in Irish folklore."

"I'm changing my mind about many beliefs, especially if it ensures your happiness."

His response made her throat ache. Her Colum, ever wanting to please her.

"The ring is perfect," she said.

"Keira Moira Murphy." Colum brushed his lips over her forehead, her cheeks, her mouth. "Will you marry me?"

"I can't wait to be your wife." She looped her fingers

around his nape. Her lips parted for his lengthy, loving kiss. "Aye. Aye. Aye."

"Let's plan a New Year's Eve wedding, if you agree."

"New Year's is only a few days from now."

"That'll do."

"Our engagement will last less than a week?"

"Our engagement has survived decades." He glanced at her cottage. "We'll make our home there."

"You'll be living with me?"

"When we're married. Aye. A place next door to our parents is ideal, as we can care for them as they grow older. We have a responsibility to ensure they are secure, protected, and we're providing the help they may require."

"It's more than a responsibility. I consider it a privilege."

"Well stated. Plus, it's convenient whenever your recipes call for a cup of sugar." He winked.

"I don't bake. I sew."

"So we'll dine at Michael D's a lot."

She smiled. "A definite improvement over my cooking."

"I remember you were never much of a cook."

"What else do you remember?"

"I recall you always fired my heart into a tailspin." He tossed her one of his lopsided smiles. "And, I remembered the vacant building in town. I located the owner, and I've secured a lease on the place adjacent to your shop. This little town needs more culture and a community theater is an excellent beginning."

"You mentioned you preferred bigger cities."

He quirked an eyebrow. "Can a man adjust his opinions, or is that a woman's prerogative?"

"Both." She laughed. "Colum O'Brien, you've made me so happy."

"Kiki, I've only just begun."

EPILOGUE

*N*ew Year's Eve day brought a brisk breeze and threat of showers. Outside, a huge white tent had been erected near the Irish Sea, and both the ceremony and reception would be held inside. Large propane portable heaters had been set up to take away the bite in the air.

Keira gave a last glance at herself in the mirror at her light-peach lace wedding dress, pleased with her appearance. The ivory netting veil with a feather and tulle flower; accented the feminine, flowing lines. She'd dipped the ends of her hair in a subtle shade of dusty yellow.

At two o'clock, the ceremony opened with the swell of keyboard music, and a hush went through the crowd. The tent glowed with candlelight, perfumed with rich bouquets of shamrock and crimson roses, tied with red satin ribbons. She savored every second, giving a special nod to her two beautiful daughters and her new friends, Patrick and Cora Gervez.

Colum had introduced her to them when they'd arrived from Farthing for the wedding, and they'd immediately invited her and Colum to America—enthusiastically chatting about their colleagues and family in Bloomingfield, California.

"You'll enjoy Julie Rossi's restaurant, The Pasta Junction, because she makes her own homemade pasta every day," Cora had gushed, as she tucked a dark-brown curl behind her ear. "Her husband, Lorenzo, is the local weatherman."

'We work together at the television studio." Patrick's blue eyes gleamed with pride as he beamed down at his wife.

Keira and Colum assured they'd love to see America.

"Perhaps for our honeymoon?" Colum asked her. "January weather in California is mild and has it all—beaches, mountains, and, from what Patrick has described—Bloomingfield Candy Shop—the finest chocolate shop in the world."

"Aye, it sounds grand," she'd replied.

As Keira started down the aisle, she carried a photo in her mind of this day—her true wedding day, exquisite and with the promise of a lifetime of love.

When she approached the altar, she grinned at her mum, her matron of honor, and Colum's father, the best man.

Then her gaze locked with her tall, handsome groom, resplendent in a dove-gray suit and emerald-green tie that matched his eyes.

Colum gazed at her with quiet joy. "Hello, my love," he whispered.

She recalled everything they'd been through, their decades apart. Love had emerged from friendship and taken hold. In harmony, their journey had led them back to exactly where they'd begun, and truly, this was the happiest of New Year's. Welcoming the future and letting go of the past, in the company of her loved ones.

With her hands laced with his, she repeated her wedding vows with him. They commenced the ceremony by reciting a traditional Irish blessing, an ancient Celtic prayer:

"May the road rise up to meet you.

May the wind be always at your back.

May the sun shine warm upon your face; the rains fall soft upon your fields and until we meet again, may God hold you in the palm of His hand."

And then she silently added to herself:

Once upon a time, there was a girl named Kiki, and a guy named Colum.

A fairytale. A happily ever after.

THE END

A NOTE FROM JOSIE

Dear Reader,

Thank you for reading *A Chocolate-Box Irish Wedding*.

I wanted to write another story loosely connected to the "Chocolate-Box" series, and located the story to Ireland during the holidays and New Year's. I chose Colum, a character from Oh Danny Boy and also brought two characters from A Chocolate-Box Christmas Wish—Cora and Patrick—to share a winter romance with you.

If you loved this sweet romance as much as I loved writing it, please help other people find *A Chocolate-Box Irish Wedding* by posting your review.

The books in the Chocolate-Box Series include:

A Chocolate-Box Christmas- Love is sweeter with a touch of mischief.

A Chocolate-Box New Years- Fresh pasta isn't the only specialty that takes extra time.

A Chocolate-Box Valentine- It's your last love who truly matters.

A Chocolate-Box Summer Breeze- It's never too late to find love again.

A Chocolate-Box Christmas Wish- He's been all over the world. She's a home-town girl. Can a holiday wish bridge the gap?

A Chocolate-Box Irish Wedding- Will their individual journeys lead them back to where it all began in beautiful Ireland?

A Chocolate-Box Irish Wedding is available in ebook, paperback, Large Print paperback, Hardcover, and audiobook.

I'd love to meet you in person someday, but in the meantime, all I can offer is a sincere and grateful thank you. Without your support, my books would not be possible.

As I write my next sweet or inspirational romance, remember this: Have you ever tried something you were afraid to try because it mattered so much to you? I did, when I started writing. Take the chance, and just do something you love.

My Spotify Play List for A Chocolate-Box Irish Wedding is here.

With sincere appreciation,

Josie Riviera

Love sweet romance holiday stories?
Be sure to check out my book bundles:
Holiday Hearts Volume One
Holiday Hearts Volume Two
Holiday Hearts Book Bundle Volume Three
Holiday Hearts Volume Four

Holiday Hearts Book Bundle Volume Five

Love the "Chocolate Box" sweet romances?
Click here.

Love Irish romances?
Irish Hearts Sweet Romance Bundle

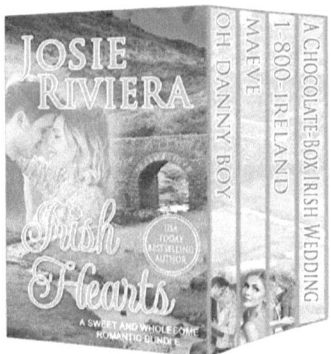

RECIPE FOR CHERYL'S IRISH
SODA BREAD

Ingredients:
    2 1/2 cups all-purpose flour
    3 tablespoons sugar
    2 teaspoons baking powder
    1 teaspoon baking soda
    1/2 teaspoon salt
    1/3 cup cold butter, cut into chunks
    1/2 cup currants or raisins
    1 1/4 cups buttermilk
Substitute 4 teaspoons vinegar or lemon juice plus enough milk to equal 1 1/4 cups. Let stand 5 minutes.

Preparation:

STEP 1

Heat oven to 375°F. Line baking sheet with parchment paper; set aside.

STEP 2

Combine all ingredients except buttermilk and currants in bowl; cut in butter until mixture resembles coarse crumbs. Stir in buttermilk and currants just until moistened.

STEP 3

Turn dough onto lightly floured surface; knead gently 10 times. Shape into a ball. Place onto the prepared baking sheet. Pat into 6-inch circle. Cut 1/2 inch deep "X" in top of dough with sharp knife.

STEP 4

Bake 30-35 minutes or until golden brown. Serve warm. Enjoy!

A CHOCOLATE-BOX CHRISTMAS
CHAPTER ONE PREVIEW

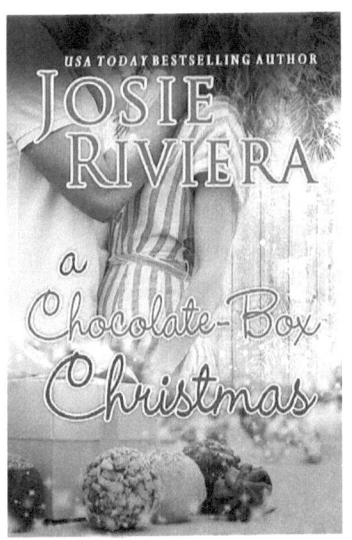

CHAPTER ONE

Maise Anderson stood at the entrance to the women's shelter in her new hometown, her gaze fastened on the front door.

The weather was a typical mid-December afternoon in California, but she was accustomed to cooler temperatures.

However, this wasn't about winter. This was about chocolate.

Under normal circumstances, she would have admired the magnificent landscape surrounding the town of Bloomingfield—the imposing snow-capped mountains, the towering ponderosa pines—but she couldn't, because all she focused on was reaching for the metal door handle and turning it.

With a nervous inhale, she gave herself a stern reminder.

You can accomplish this simple assignment. Candy is a sweet holiday treat. Besides, everyone loves chocolate.

Maybe. Maybe not.

She hadn't eaten chocolate in over two years because of a nasty bout of food poisoning.

Nonetheless, she hadn't gotten sick because of the chocolate, she rationalized, as she recalled that particular dining assignment. Most likely, she'd gotten sick because of her entrée.

She flicked a glance toward the leaden sky, grimacing when a brisk wind blew misty rain across her face. A chill rose up her neck and she shivered.

She tucked her small umbrella under her arm and pressed her lips together.

Outwardly, she passed for the ideal food critic. Her shoulder-length chestnut hair was pulled into a classic chignon, her beige leather pumps sported a sensible heel, and her camel-colored blazer was tasteful and practical. She'd opted for tailored navy-blue slacks, topped with an emerald-green turtleneck sweater, holiday looking but conservative. She'd kept her makeup to a minimum—muted red lipstick, a light rosy blush, and mascara to highlight her green eyes.

Confidence and expertise on the outside. Foreboding and anxiety on the inside.

She blew out a whoosh of air, straightened her shoulders, and pushed open the door to the shelter. "Here we go," she said under her breath. "I can withstand anything for an hour."

"Happy holidays, Miss Anderson." The mayor, Ed Johnson, a thin man but with a wide grin to make up for it, hailed her as she stepped inside. They'd met at a Hometown Holiday event at the County Museum the previous weekend. "There's a cold front coming in. I'm pleased you agreed to judge our annual fund-raiser."

"I'm happy to participate," she lied. In reality, she had no choice. Her boss, the editor of *Bloomingfield Daily Dispatch*, had given her the assignment with a gruff, "There's no food budget for this affair. Take a couple of pictures with your phone camera, sample the weirdest piece of chocolate you can find, and follow up with a full-of-praise article."

Such was the job of a food-writer reporter. No extravagant feast or fancy sushi. Just pure, sweet chocolate.

*** End of Excerpt A Chocolate-Box Christmas by Josie Riviera ***

Want more? Keep reading A Chocolate-Box Christmas.
Available on Amazon! FREE on Kindle Unlmited

Or grab Chocolate-Box Double Hearts here.
All six "Chocolate-Box" books in 1 sweet bundle.

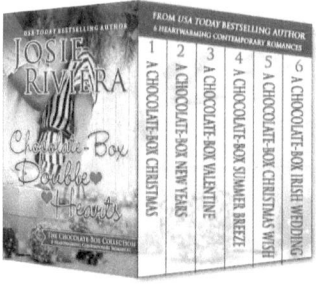

FREE on Kindle Unlimited.

ABOUT THE AUTHOR

Josie Riviera is a *USA TODAY* bestselling author of contemporary, inspirational, and historical sweet romances that read like Hallmark movies. She lives in the Charlotte, NC, area with her wonderfully supportive husband. They share their home with an adorable shih tzu, who constantly needs grooming, and live in an old house forever needing renovations.

To receive my Newsletter and your free sweet romance novella ebook as a thank you gift, sign up HERE.

Become a member of my Read and Review VIP Facebook group for exclusive giveaways and FREE ARC's.

josieriviera.com/

ACKNOWLEDGMENTS

An appreciative thank you to my patient husband, Dave, and our three wonderful children.

ALSO BY JOSIE RIVIERA

Seeking Patience

Seeking Catherine (always Free!)

Seeking Fortune

Seeking Charity

Seeking Rachel

The Seeking Series

Oh Danny Boy

I Love You More

A Snowy White Christmas

A Portuguese Christmas

Holiday Hearts Book Bundle Volume One

Holiday Hearts Book Bundle Volume Two

Holiday Hearts Book Bundle Volume Three

Holiday Hearts Book Bundle Volume Four

Holiday Hearts Book Bundle Volume Five

Candleglow and Mistletoe

Maeve (Perfect Match)

A Love Song To Cherish

A Christmas To Cherish

A Valentine To Cherish

A Christmas Puppy To Cherish

A Homecoming To Cherish

A Summer To Cherish

Romance Stories To Cherish

Romance Stories To Cherish Volume Two

Cherished Hearts Six Book Volume

Aloha To Love

Sweet Peppermint Kisses

Valentine Hearts Boxed Set

1-800-CUPID

1-800-CHRISTMAS

1-800-IRELAND

1-800-SUMMER

1-800-NEW YEAR

Irish Hearts Sweet Romance Bundle

Holly's Gift

A Chocolate-Box Christmas

A Chocolate-Box New Years

A Chocolate-Box Valentine

A Chocolate-Box Summer Breeze

A Chocolate-Box Christmas Wish

A Chocolate-Box Irish Wedding

Chocolate-Box Hearts

Chocolate-Box Hearts Volume Two

Chocolate-Box Double Hearts

Recipes From The Heart

Leading Hearts

New Year Hearts

SENIOR HEARTS

Summer Hearts

Christmas in the Air (1-800-Book)

A Very Christian Christmas

The 1-800-Series Volume Two

The 1-800-Series Complete

Christmas Tails of the Heart

Cocoa's Christmas Love

Pawfect Christmas Hearts

Pink Coral Island

Most books are available in ebook, audiobook, paperback, Large Print paperback and Hardcover.

Many are FREE on Kindle Unlimited!